Let your dreams take flight
with this book that belongs to

Gracious

Published by Scholastic Inc., 90 Old Sherman Turnpike,
Danbury, Connecticut 06816.

For information regarding permission, write to:
Disney Licensed Publishing, 114 Fifth Avenue, New York, New York 10011.

978-0-7172-8328-6
0-7172-8328-3

Printed in the U.S.A.
First printing, December 2007

WALT DISNEY

Peter Pan

SCHOLASTIC INC.

New York Toronto London Auckland Sydney
Mexico City New Delhi Hong Kong Buenos Aires

Wendy Darling and her brothers, John and little Michael, were restless. It was almost bedtime, but the boys weren't sleepy at all.

The two brothers were playing pirates and Indians.

But tonight, they got into trouble. They had
drawn a pirate map on their father's shirt. He was
very upset and told Wendy that it would be her last
night in the nursery.

To cheer up the boys, Wendy began to tell them stories about Peter Pan and Never Land.

Outside the nursery's window sat Peter Pan and Tinker Bell. Peter had always enjoyed sitting outside the window and listening to Wendy's stories. On his last visit, however, he had lost his shadow; and tonight, he came to find it.

Tinker Bell, who had snuck into the nursery, came out to tell Peter that she had found his shadow.

Peter Pan and Tinker Bell flew in through the
nursery window.

"I saved your shadow for you," Wendy said.

"It needs sewing," she pointed out. "That's the proper way to do it."

As Wendy mended Peter's shadow, she told him that this would be her last night in the nursery.

"I won't have it! Come on," exclaimed Peter as he took Wendy's hand, "to Never Land!"

"But Peter, how do we get to Never Land?" asked Wendy, surprised.

"Fly, of course. All you have to do is think of a wonderful thought."

Wendy, John, and Michael thought of toys and sleighbells and a mermaid lagoon, but still they couldn't fly.

Peter encouraged them. "All it takes is faith and trust," he said, "and something I forgot—dust!"

Peter sprinkled some of Tinker Bell's magical pixie dust on Wendy, John, and Michael. Soon everyone, except their dog, was flying away to Never Land, despite Michael's best efforts.

"Oh, Peter, it's just as I've always dreamed it would be," Wendy said with a sigh, as she looked down at the magical island.

"There's the Indian camp!" yelled John.

"And there's a pirate ship," cried Michael.

The captain of the pirate ship was Peter's greatest enemy: Captain Hook. He had lost his left hand fighting Peter when a hungry crocodile had swallowed it during the fight.

Since then, Captain Hook devoted all his time to trying to catch Peter Pan. Hook would do *anything* to get his revenge.

All of a sudden Peter, Tink, Wendy, and the boys heard a loud boom! A cannonball had zoomed past them! Captain Hook had spotted Peter Pan and started firing the ship's guns.

"Quick, Tink!" Peter yelled. "Take Wendy
and the boys to the island. I'll stay here and draw
Hook's fire."

Tinker Bell flew off, not waiting for Wendy and
her brothers. Tink was jealous of Wendy and all the
attention she was getting from Peter.

Once Tink reached the island, she found the
Lost Boys, Peter Pan's friends in Never Land. She
delivered a message that a terrible "Wendy-bird"
was heading their way. Peter wanted this awful
bird shot down.

"Let's go!" they said.

As soon as the Lost Boys spotted Wendy, they aimed their slingshots and fired rocks at her, knocking Wendy down!

But Peter arrived just in time to catch Wendy.
Peter was furious at the Lost Boys.

"Well, Tink said it was a bird," said one boy
named Cubby.

"She said you said to shoot it down," added
another boy named Rabbit.

"You might have killed her," Peter scolded Tinker Bell, "I hereby banish you forever," Peter declared. But then he changed his mind and banished Tink for a week.

Peter then took Wendy to show her Mermaid
Lagoon.

John and Michael went to look for Indians. The
Lost Boys declared John the leader. They all lined up
behind him and marched through the jungle.

The boys didn't notice all the mysterious bushes and trees following them. Without warning, a group of Indians leapt out from behind the trees and grabbed them!

The Indians tied up the boys and took them to their village where the Indian Chief was waiting.

"Where'd you hide Princess Tiger Lily?" the Chief demanded.

"We ain't got your old princess!" the boys replied. But the Chief didn't believe them.

Meanwhile, Peter and Wendy spotted Captain Hook and Smee in a small boat. They had captured Princess Tiger Lily!

Hook held Tiger Lily prisoner and tied her down to a rock in the sea.

Peter flew down to rescue Tiger Lily. He used a clever voice imitation to make Smee release Tiger Lily.

Captain Hook and Peter began fighting. But Peter was much too quick for the Captain.

Unfortunately for Hook, the crocodile that had once swallowed the pirate's hand suddenly appeared.

Hook was no match for Peter. The Captain fell into the water. The crocodile had been waiting for this chance!

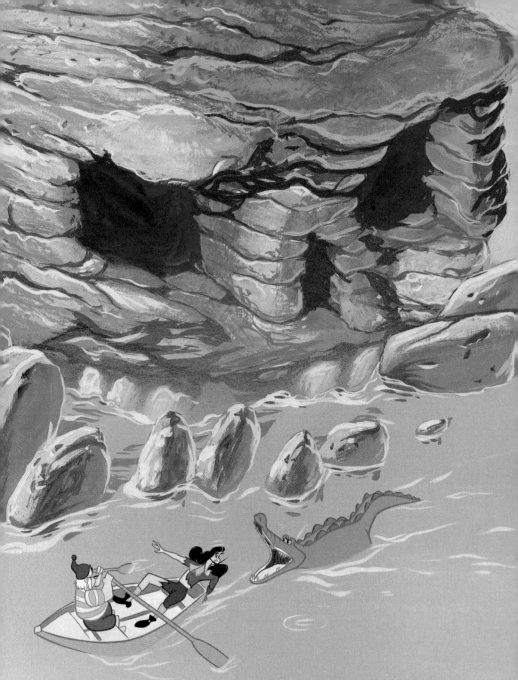

Frantic, Hook yelled for help as the crocodile
chased after him. "Smee!" Hook yelped. "Save me!"

With the pirates busy, Peter quickly untied Tiger Lily and brought her back to the village. The Chief was happy to have his daughter home. He freed John, Michael, and the Lost Boys. He then placed a headdress on Peter in gratitude for rescuing Tiger Lily.

Tinker Bell was still resentful of Wendy. Tink had flown off by herself and was captured by Smee! Smee brought Tink to Captain Hook.

Captain Hook promised to take Wendy away to sea if Tinker Bell would say where Wendy was.

Tinker Bell fell for Hook's evil plan and showed him how to reach Peter's secret hideaway.

Meanwhile, Wendy
and her brothers wanted
to go home. The Lost
Boys wanted to join them.
But Peter wanted them
to stay in Never Land. He
was upset, so he stayed
behind in his hideout.

But Hook's men were
outside waiting for them.
The pirates captured
Wendy and the boys!

After the pirates tied the boys up,
Hook decided to send a special package
to Peter—a package that would blast
Peter out of Never Land forever!

The pirates took Wendy
and the boys to the ship.
Captain Hook wanted them to
become pirates.

"Come on, join up!" he said.
"And I'll be frank—unless you
do, you'll walk the plank!"

Tinker Bell knew she had to
get Peter to save them. She broke
free and flew quickly to Peter's
secret hideout.

Peter was just about to open his package from
Captain Hook when Tink flew in. She tried to pull
the package away, but Peter kept tugging at it. She
finally pushed the box as far from Peter as she could.

The box began smoking and moments
later . . . *ka-boom!* The box exploded!

Back on the ship, Captain Hook was demanding
an answer. "Which will it be," asked Hook, as he
held up a contract, "the pen or the plank?"

"Peter Pan will save us," Wendy whispered to the
boys. Then she bravely announced to Hook
as she walked onto the plank, "We will never join
your crew!"

She took the last step off the plank. . . .
Everyone waited for the splash. But
Peter Pan arrived just in time to catch
Wendy as she fell.

Peter took Wendy to a safe place. He then returned to fight Captain Hook.

The two fought while the children and the pirates watched. As always, Peter was much quicker and smarter than the Captain.

Hook jabbed his sword at Peter. The Captain eventually lost his balance—much to the delight of the hungry crocodile below. Hook fell into the sea with a big splash!

Once the pirates saw that Peter had defeated their captain, they gave up the fight and abandoned ship. Everyone cheered for Peter Pan.

"Michael! John!" said Wendy, "We're going home!" At Peter Pan's command, Tinker Bell flew all around the ship, sprinkling her magical pixie dust. Moments later the ship was glowing like gold and flew into the sky.

Soon after, Mr. and Mrs. Darling found
Wendy asleep by the nursery's window.
"Wendy," Mrs. Darling called out.
"Mother, we're back!" exclaimed Wendy.
"Back?" asked Mr. Darling.

While the boys were asleep,
Wendy told her parents of their
adventures in Never Land.
"It was an amazing adventure
with mermaids, pirates,
and we flew in the sky!"
exclaimed Wendy.

Mr. Darling looked up into the night sky. There, he saw a ship made of clouds crossing the moon.

"I have the strangest feeling that I've seen that ship before," Mr. Darling said, remembering his own boyhood. "A long time ago, when I was very young."

And, indeed, he had.

Eye Spy

Travel back to
Never Land and
see if you can find
these pictures.